ANZAC
BOYS

ANZAC BOYS

TONY BRADMAN

With illustrations by
Ollie Cuthbertson

Barrington  Stoke

First published in 2015 in Great Britain by
Barrington Stoke Ltd
18 Walker Street, Edinburgh, EH3 7LP

www.barringtonstoke.co.uk

And the Band Played Waltzing Matilda – words and music by
Eric Bogle. Used courtesy of Domino Publishing Company Ltd.

Text © 2015 Tony Bradman
Illustrations © 2015 Ollie Cuthbertson

A CIP catalogue record for this book is available
from the British Library upon request

ISBN: 978-1-78112-434-5

Printed in China by Leo

For all the Barkers, wherever they may be

CONTENTS

PART 1
ORPHANS
1906

CHAPTER 1

When I Was a Young Man

The gluey grey porridge was growing cold in its bowl.

"Come on, Frank, eat up," I whispered. "We don't want to get in trouble again. Father Murphy said it's a sin to waste good food."

Me and my brother Frank were sitting at a table in the dining hall of the orphanage. It was a large room with a high ceiling and there were three long, narrow tables down the middle. A hundred boys in thick grey shirts and trousers sat on the hard benches that ran down either side. Most of us were spooning up porridge from our bowls as fast as we could, but Frank had barely touched his.

"It's slimy," he complained. "It makes me feel sick." He puffed out his cheeks and made gagging noises.

"Ssshhh!" I snapped. "Just swallow it before you get us both in trouble." I looked round, but Father Sullivan, the priest on breakfast duty, didn't seem to have heard.

"Stop telling me what to do." Frank scowled and chucked his spoon down. "I'm not going to eat this muck, and you can't make me."

That was the trouble with Frank – he could be dead awkward sometimes. Some boys near by glanced at us, and Father Sullivan turned to look as well. But at that moment the doors of the dining hall slammed open and Father Darcy strode in.

"Bert and Frank Barker?" he bellowed. His narrow eyes scanned the room. I jumped up from the bench and pulled Frank with me. Father Darcy's gaze locked onto us. "Father Murphy wants to see you," he snapped. "Well, what are you waiting for?"

Father Darcy turned on his heel and strode out. I was worried now. Father Murphy was the priest in charge. As I hurried after Father Darcy, dragging Frank along, I panicked but I couldn't think of what we had done to make Father Murphy cross.

We'd been in the orphanage a month. Before that, we lived with our mum in Kentish Town. Our dad had died when Frank was a baby, and life had been hard ever since. Mum worked in a laundry, but her wages only just covered our rent. We were poor, but we managed. I did my best to help Mum – keeping Frank from under her feet and running errands. The three of us were happy. And then Mum got sick.

She got the sack from her laundry job, and then there was no money to pay for a doctor. Mum had done a lot of praying instead, and she'd dragged herself to Mass every Sunday. But she died anyway. God and His saints let her down. There was nobody to take in Frank and me, so our priest packed us off to St Patrick's orphanage. It had been a bit of a shock, to say the least. First our mum was torn away from us, and then we found ourselves dumped in this huge, cold building with a hundred other waifs and strays.

It was a terrible place. We all had to wear a uniform of grey shirts and trousers, and they itched like mad. We slept in cold, bare dorms with a dozen beds in each. They woke us at six every morning for Mass, and we spent the rest of the day in lessons. There were bullies, and fights, and anything we had got nicked. But the worst thing of all was the priests.

The priests prowled around at all hours of the day and night in their long black cassocks, like giant ravens who might eat you alive. Some of them enjoyed whacking boys on the backside or round the head. If a boy talked back or gave them cheek, they locked him in a cupboard for hours, or beat him with a heavy leather strap.

At night the dorms were full of the sound of sobbing.

So, I suppose it would be fair to say I didn't much like the orphanage. But Frank hated the place. I was old enough to understand I had to keep my thoughts to myself, but Frank couldn't keep his trap shut. He was always getting told off for complaining. He hadn't got the strap yet, but I knew it was only a matter of time before he did. I spent my whole life making excuses for him and protecting him from the other boys – and the priests. And then I had to comfort him at night when he cried.

I didn't really mind. We were family, and we had no one but each other. We both missed our mum so much, and Frank couldn't help being the way he was. He hated people telling him what to do. He had this way of looking straight at you that really rattled the priests – and so they looked for any excuse to take out their anger on him. He was an easy target. I was 12, almost a grown-up, but he was only 9. I look tough – dark, with brown eyes, and small for my age, but stocky. Mum always said I wouldn't grow tall because we never had enough food. But that didn't seem to have held Frank back. He was already as tall as me, but skinny, and fair, and soft-looking.

As we walked along the corridor that day behind Father Darcy, I turned to look at Frank as he tried to keep up on his long, spindly legs. His bottom lip was trembling, and his face was pale. I had to do something to make him feel better. I didn't know then that what I was about to say would come back to haunt me. To haunt both of us.

"Listen, Frank, don't worry – whatever happens I promise I'll always take care of you." I kept my voice low so Father Darcy wouldn't hear – he had a sharp tongue and a quick temper. "We'll be fine so long as we're together," I whispered.

Frank glanced at me and nodded, swallowing hard.

Just then we arrived at Father Murphy's study. Father Darcy opened the door and ushered us inside. The study was lined with glass-fronted bookcases full of leather-covered volumes, and it had a window with a view onto the garden. Father Murphy was sitting at his desk, a cross on the wall behind him. Below the cross was a jewel-coloured picture of Mary and the baby Jesus. It made me think of my mum and I bit my tongue, hard.

Father Murphy looked up. He had cold blue eyes and a thatch of silver hair brushed back from his forehead. His lips were thin and stern

and he never smiled. On bad days, I thought God himself probably looked like Father Murphy. Me and Frank stood before him and my heart hammered away in fear.

"Thank you, Father Darcy," Father Murphy said. His voice was deep, his Irish accent strong. "Well, boys," he said. "I have something very important to tell you. We've been thinking about your case, and it has been decided your future lies elsewhere."

"Sorry, Father?" I stuttered. "I'm not sure what you mean."

"It's simple," Father Murphy said. "We were more than happy to take you boys in here at St Patrick's when your poor mother died, God rest her soul."

"God rest her soul indeed, Father," Father Darcy broke in, and he crossed himself.

"But now we'll be sending you to another place," Father Murphy said.

"Another place, Father?" I said. "Where?"

"Australia," Father Murphy said. "You'll be leaving in three days."

CHAPTER 2

The Ship Pulled Away

Australia?

I wasn't sure I'd heard right. Australia was on the other side of the world! Frank and me had only ever been out of London once, and that was on a day trip with Mum to the seaside at Southend. 40 miles away.

"You don't look impressed," Father Murphy said. His voice was stern and he scowled at us. "You should be grateful, boys. This is a marvellous chance for poor boys like you. You won't get another one like it."

"We are grateful, aren't we?" I said, and I nudged Frank. He didn't respond. "For everything, that is," I added. "Sorry."

"I'm glad to hear it," Father Murphy growled. He leaned forward with his elbows on his desk and his hands clasped. "Now, I'm sure you boys haven't given much thought to your future. Boys never think past dinner time, do they, Father Darcy?"

"They're too busy getting up to mischief," said the other priest.

"Quite," said Father Murphy. "It's mischief that's the problem, right enough. We're taking excellent care of you now, boys. But we won't always be around to keep you on the straight and narrow. When you leave the Church's care, that's when you might fall into bad habits ... We've seen it happen too often. Boys are easily led, and big cities like London are nests of crime and vice, full of every kind of sin."

"They are indeed," said Father Darcy, and he made the sign of the cross.

I had a good idea of what Father Murphy was talking about. You can't grow up in London and not see plenty of sin. There were thieves and drunks and all sorts of goings-on on the street where we grew up. I'd already decided to steer clear of all that – it never seemed to end well. But somehow Father Murphy made me feel guilty anyway.

"So to keep you safe, the Church has come up with a plan to send boys like you out to the New World," Father Murphy said. "There's work for you there – you can learn to be farmers and live clean, decent lives. That's good for you, of course, and it will help keep the Empire strong. Australia needs as many boys from here as possible – fresh, young lads to help keep it Christian. We're sending a few boys to start with, so you'll be the first to have this wonderful adventure." He beamed at us for a second. "That's all for now," he said. "Father Darcy will explain the rest."

But all Father Darcy did was give us some books about Australia from the library. That night, I sat with Frank on his bed before lights-out and we flicked through the pages. We both liked the pictures of the funny-looking animals like kangaroos and wallabies and possums and dingos. There were pictures of deserts, too, and farms with herds of cattle and flocks of sheep. It looked hot and dusty, and the land stretched as far as the eye could see. Not like damp, cramped, dirty London.

One of the books had a map at the back that showed the world spread over two pages. Large parts of it were in red to show they belonged to the British Empire.

"This is Britain," I told Frank, and I pointed to a cluster of islands at the top of the map. "London is the little black dot ... all this blue stuff is the sea ..." I moved my finger across the sea to show him the route I thought we would take. "And this is Australia," I finished.

Frank peered at where I was pointing. "What are those?" he asked, and he jabbed a finger at some small red blobs in the blue sea, even further on than Australia.

I turned the book so I could see. "New Zealand," I read. I'd never heard of the place before, and I didn't think much about it then. I had no idea that these islands at the edge of the world would play such a big part in our lives.

Frank stared at the map in silence. Then he looked up at me, and his blue eyes were wet with tears. "I don't want to go to Australia, Bert," he said. "It's too far away."

The idea of going to Australia scared me as well, but I couldn't admit that to Frank. "What are you worried about?" I said, and I forced a smile. "Father Murphy wouldn't send us anywhere bad. You heard what he said – it's going to be an adventure."

And there was a part of me that wanted to know more about this vast, hot land where we were going – more than we could learn from a few library books.

"Well, if you say so," Frank murmured. "And we'll be together, won't we?"

"Of course we will." I ruffled his hair. "Now go to sleep."

Three days later we left the orphanage in a horse and cart with Father Darcy. All we had was a small bag each with a few bits and pieces of spare clothing. The ship to Australia would leave from Southampton, and we would take a train from Waterloo to get there. That meant we got a last good look at London, with its shops and monuments and crowds of people. The station was crowded too, full of noise and smoke from the trains.

"Look at that!" Frank said. His eyes shone with excitement. He pointed at a steam engine, a massive gleaming monster of black iron. He was right – it was an amazing sight. I couldn't help starting to feel excited too.

But once we were on board, the train journey seemed to go on for ever. At last we arrived in Southampton. Father Darcy led us out of the station into the busy streets.

"How much further is it, Father?" Frank asked. "When will we …"

He fell silent. We turned a corner and there before us was a huge ship. It towered over the harbour, and its two funnels rose into the evening sky. People were walking up a narrow gangway to the deck, where men in uniforms waited. I'd seen pictures of sailors in one of those library books and I felt a thrill at the sight of their peaked caps and brass buttons. The ship's name was painted on the side – SS *Southern Star*.

"Father Darcy! Over here!"

The three of us looked over and saw a short, bald man standing close to the ship, shouting and waving at us. Father Darcy waved back, then took us over to him.

A group of boys stood behind the man. One of them shoved the boy beside him, then pointed at Frank and me and smirked.

"They're all yours, Father Simpkins," Father Darcy said, and he pushed us towards the other priest.

The two priests shook hands, then without a word to us, Father Darcy turned and strode away.

"Right, boys, that's everybody," Father Simpkins said. "Up you go, then."

An hour later, the SS *Southern Star* set sail for Australia.

CHAPTER 3

Weary Weeks

It turned out the boys with Father Simpkins were from orphanages from all over the country. There were 30 of us in the group now that Frank and me had joined them. A sailor took us all deep down into the dark bowels of the ship, to the cabin we'd share for the crossing. It wasn't much bigger than Father Murphy's study at St Patrick's, and it was packed full of metal bunk beds. Damp ran off the steel walls.

"I'll leave you boys to settle in," Father Simpkins said. "Behave yourselves."

The instant his back was turned all hell broke loose, as everyone shoved each other out of the way to get to the bunks they wanted. I stayed where I was. I'd already picked the bunk closest to the door, and I chucked my bag onto the bottom bed. If we got it, I would have a chance of getting Frank out if we ran into a storm at sea and the ship sank. Although I wasn't sure what we'd do after that.

"I think you'll find I've got first dibs on that, pal," said a big lad with a broad northern accent. "So why don't you just tootle off and find yourself another?"

He folded his arms and a few other boys came to stand behind him, all trying their hardest to look tough. The boy came closer. He was older and bigger than me, and I could see he was the kind of lad who liked a scrap. My heart started thumping. Things could get very tricky for Frank and me if I showed weakness now.

So I stood my ground. "Thanks, but we like these two," I said, and I clenched my fists.

The boy paused as he took the measure of me. Everybody held their breath for a few seconds. Then at last the boy shrugged and grinned, and his air of menace vanished. "You're a right stubborn bugger, aren't you, and no mistake," he said. "Fair enough, those bunks are yours. I'm Stanley, by the way. Let me introduce you to the rest of the lads ..."

They were a right bunch of ragamuffins. Their clothes didn't fit, and some of them had on stuff that was so old, it was almost rags. There were lots of different accents, too. Scotland, the North of England, the Midlands, the West Country, even a couple from Ireland. I found it hard to understand some of them. But they said the same about me, with my London accent.

"Come on, let's have a look round the ship," a boy called Lenny said. He was thin and weedy, as if he hadn't had a decent meal in his life.

"But Father Simpkins told us we had to stay here," I said.

"Stuff Father Simpkins," Stanley said. "He don't care about us."

That shocked me for a minute, but there wasn't time to think about it too much. Stanley led us out of the cabin, and we all went off to explore. Frank and me tagged along with Stanley and Lenny. To begin with I expected Father Simpkins to appear out of nowhere and tell us off, but that didn't happen. And then the ship turned out to be so interesting that I stopped worrying.

Within a few days we had explored every inch of it. It was a world all of its own. The Captain ran things from the bridge, the crew carried out his orders, and the passengers were divided into classes, just like people back at home. The first-class passengers had their own section of the ship, with dining rooms and cabins and all sorts of comforts that we never got near. The second class had cabins that weren't so posh, and the third class – the poor people – had to muck in together.

"We're lowest of the low," Stanley said one day, as we watched a first-class family stroll out onto an upper deck. "They'd say we're scum."

I had a feeling Stanley was right. But we all got on fine with the third-class passengers and the crew. We even made friends with the stokers in the engine rooms. One of them found some trousers and shirts for the boys with the worst clothes, and they gave us other things too. Food, cigarette cards – nothing much, but more than most of us had ever had before. But the first- and second-class passengers looked down their noses at us and they complained about us too.

Father Simpkins didn't take any notice of
the complaints. Stanley was right about him as
well – he didn't care about us at all. He had a
second-class cabin, but he spent most of his time
in the ship's bar, drinking whisky, smoking and
playing cards. He only visited our cabin twice in
the six long weeks of the voyage.

There were rough seas in the Bay of Biscay,
and there was lots of seasickness on board, but
Frank and me felt fine. The Mediterranean was
calm – blue and sparkling, the sun growing hotter
every day. We sailed down the great Suez Canal,
where the land was dry and brown on both sides.
Then we entered the Red Sea, which wasn't red,
and crossed the Indian Ocean to Ceylon.

The ship stopped for a day at Colombo, a port
in Ceylon. Frank and me went up to the main
deck to escape the smell of sweaty bodies in our
cabin. The bustling harbour spread out beneath
us, with its clatter and yells.

I was amazed at how dark-skinned the people
were. But then Frank and me had turned almost
as brown on the voyage. The food on the ship
had been all right too, and I had never seen

Frank looking so healthy, or so happy. His legs had got even longer, but they weren't so skinny any more.

"I wish we could get off the ship for a bit," said Frank. "We wouldn't get lost, would we?"

But Father Simpkins left the bar for long enough to forbid any boy to leave the ship.

"We can't," I said. "We'll be in Australia soon anyway."

Two weeks later we arrived in Western Australia. By then I was glad to say goodbye to the *Southern Star*. Father Simpkins led us across the harbour to a huge shed full of people. He pushed and shoved his way through and we followed as best we could. At last he found two priests who had come to meet us.

"Right, boys, we'll get the papers signed and be on our way," Father Simpkins said. An official-looking man checked and signed a pile of papers, and at last we got out of the shed. There were dozens of carts and carriages waiting to take people away. Father Simpkins and the priests led us over to two large horse-drawn carts. Long shadows were creeping over the dusty ground and the sun was setting over the harbour.

Father Simpkins split us into two groups, one for each cart. He separated me from Frank. Frank didn't like that idea, and he hung on to me.

"Come on, boy, we haven't got all day," Father Simpkins said. His face turned even redder as he dragged Frank off me and set him in the other cart.

"We have to do as we're told," I shouted to Frank, but he started to cry.

When both carts were full we set off. We went past some warehouses and a railway station, then a few miles further on we came to a place where the road split in two. The cart I was in swung to the left, and Frank's to the right. I watched in horror as Frank's cart vanished into the gloom.

It was a week before they told me my brother had been sent to New Zealand.

PART 2
EXILES
1907–1914

CHAPTER 4

The Dusty Outback

I sat in the corridor outside the office of Father McTavish, the Principal of St Wilfred's, and felt my stomach churn. I knew he wouldn't listen to me, but I had to try.

"Come in," a voice called. I trudged over and opened the door.

It was like Father Murphy's room in London. There were bookcases and a cross on the wall. But the picture was of Jesus on his own. No mothers here.

Father McTavish sat at his desk and watched me as I walked in. He was a big, beefy man with heavy jowls, speckled with stubble. I stopped in front of the desk as Father O'Flanagan walked in behind me. "Stand up straight, boy," he snapped. I pulled my shoulders back. We called Father

O'Flanagan the "Holy Terror" and it didn't pay to upset him.

Father McTavish frowned. "What's this I hear about you still carrying on, er ..." He looked down at the papers on his desk to find my name. "Bert? You should have got yourself sorted out by now, my lad. You've been here two months."

It had taken me and the other boys from the *Southern Star* a week to get to our new home. St Wilfred's was an orphanage 80 miles north of Perth. As Stanley said, it was "in the middle of nowhere" – the nearest town was a 2-hour cart ride away. But St Wilfred's had a farm school where the boys worked, growing the food the priests needed to feed us.

There were hundreds of boys at St Wilfred's, all of them from Britain. Most of the priests in charge were Australian, and a few were Irish. It was a tough place, even tougher than St Patrick's in London. The beatings there made the strap at St Patrick's look like a kiss from your mother. But by now it was hard to care. The sun shone every day, but my world was grey.

Father O'Flanagan interrupted my thoughts. "He's a right misery," he told Father McTavish. "He's still moping about his brother."

"I see," Father McTavish murmured. He glanced down at the papers again. "Your brother ... Frank is better off in New Zealand. It's not for you to disagree with what the Church has decided."

Father O'Flanagan smacked the back of my head.

"But I promised I'd take care of him and that we'd always be together," I gabbled. "He's too small to cope on his own."

"But he isn't on his own, is he?" said Father McTavish. "He's being taken care of by the Church. We know what's best for you boys. Frank will thank us for it some day, and I'm sure you will too."

"If I could write to him?" I begged. "Then he could write to me, and ..."

"Oh no, I'm afraid we can't allow that," Father McTavish said. He leaned back in his seat and gave me a look. "It's best to make it a clean break," he said. "If you write to your brother, it'll make it harder for him to settle into his new life. He'll be well on his way to forgetting you, and you must do the same."

And with that, Father McTavish dismissed me. Father O'Flanagan shoved me out the door with another clip round my ear.

I trudged off to the toilets and shut myself in. Everyone else was at the farm school, or in lessons, but I wanted to be alone. I couldn't believe they had taken my brother away from me and I couldn't stand to think of Frank, scared and alone. I wanted to lash out, smash something, scream at the top of my voice.

But I couldn't. At last, anger gave way to tears, and after that I calmed down.

I knew it was my job to be there when Frank was worried or frightened. I knew Frank didn't want to forget me. But what could I do? Nothing. I couldn't go to New Zealand – I couldn't even go to the nearest town. And Father McTavish wouldn't tell me where Frank was, and so I couldn't write to him either.

Maybe some day Frank and I would meet again. But for now I'd just have to accept the

way things were – and hope Father McTavish was right when he said that Frank was being looked after.

For the next few weeks I tried to put Frank out of my mind. But I couldn't keep Frank out of my dreams. I used to dream of the map Frank and I had looked at in the book, back in London. The map was much bigger in my dream, the colours brighter, and I could see Frank far below, in a tiny cart moving across Australia, then in a ship sailing to New Zealand. But after that, nothing. I had no idea where he was.

The weeks turned into months, and the months into years. Life at St Wilfred's was always the same, but I was glad to have mates like Stanley and Lenny. The three of us looked out for each other. We were all good with our fists and the other boys learned to leave us alone. We spent most of our days on the farm, learning about digging and planting, milking cows and shearing sheep and feeding chickens.

It was all right.

Sometimes boys from St Wilfred's were sent on loan to other farmers in the district. The farmers needed help, and it suited the priests fine not to have to feed us. So one day, in the second year, Stanley, Lenny and me were sent to three different farms, miles from each other.

I can hardly remember that year. I worked from dawn to dusk for a dour, mean farmer who treated me like a slave. I slept in a filthy old shed with a tin roof, so it was boiling inside in summer and freezing in winter. I never set foot in the house, and if I ever gave any lip, the farmer thrashed me with a stick.

"Take that, you little guttersnipe!" he would yell at me. "You're scum, that's what you are, scum from a London street."

When he beat me, I thought of those library books Father Murphy had given us back in London. I remembered looking at those animals and dreaming of our new life. The only time I saw a kangaroo or a possum, it was dead. The farmer hunted them for their meat and skins. He put poison out for the dingos and he shot them on sight.

He was a brute, and the only time I was happy was at the sheep-shearing, when bands of men came to do the work. They were wild and jolly and they taught me to shear a sheep before the beast even realised I'd got hold of it. The aboriginals who worked for the farmer were all right, but they kept themselves to themselves. The farmer was even crueller to them than he was to me.

Nobody cared if I lived or died.

There were moments I wasn't sure that I cared myself.

CHAPTER 5

Ramblin'

The years went by, and I was sent to other farms,
some better and some worse. I got used to the
life and grew strong and wiry, my skin burned
brown by the sun. Every so often I thought about
Frank, about how he was getting on in New
Zealand and whether he remembered his big
brother in Australia. But then I would feel sick
with guilt that I had let him go, and I would force
myself to think of something else.

One day, when I'd turned 16, I got a letter.

Dear Bert Barker

*As you have now reached the age of
sixteen, you are no longer in the care
of St Wilfred's Orphanage or the Holy*

37

*Catholic Church. We wish you all the best
for your future.*

I was on my own. The Church wasn't in charge
of me any more. They wouldn't send me to any
more farms, and they didn't want me back at the
orphanage. I was free to do what I wanted.

What did I want to do? I'd need a job to
survive. So I asked the farmer if he would take
me on as a farmhand.

"You've got to be jokin'," he said, laughing at
me. "I can't afford to pay you. And why should I?
I can just get another boy from the orphanage."

The farmer's words filled me with panic.
It dawned on me that none of the farmers I'd
worked for had ever paid me a wage. I knew a lot
about farming, but there were plenty of blokes
around who knew plenty more. I had no other
trade, nothing to fall back on – what if I couldn't
get a job at all? There was only one thing for it –
I'd have to ask Stanley for help.

I set off before dawn the next day for a long,
hot walk across the bush to the place Stanley
was working. Dingos howled in the heat, and

at one point I felt sure that a pack of them was following me. But just before the sun went down, I made it to the farm where Stanley was living.

"Sorry, mate, we're both in the same boat," Stanley said. He had a proper Aussie twang these days, but then so did I. "I got a letter like that a while back," he said. "But the farmer here's not such a bad bloke. He can't pay me, but he's letting me stay till I find something else."

The farmer let me stay for a few days, too. Then another farmer offered Stanley and me work for a month, and after that we found work on another farm, and another. It was tough, but at least we were free.

Two years went by and me and Stanley worked on farms all over Western Australia. We herded cattle and sheep, we brought in the harvest and made hay, we slept in bunkhouses and sometimes under the stars with the other farmhands. On a farm up north, we met a bunch of hard-looking men who'd just finished a 1,000-mile cattle drive. We were amazed to discover that one of them was our old mate Lenny.

We didn't recognise him at first – there was no sign of the thin, weedy boy we remembered. He was tall and broad now and could ride a horse like he'd been born in the saddle. That evening, the three of us sat and talked in the shade of an old gum tree by a wide, slow-flowing river.

"Strewth, Len, what happened to you?" said Stanley. "You're a bloomin' giant."

"Gerroff," said Lenny. His Aussie accent was even stronger than ours. "I suppose I always just asked for seconds at dinner," he joked. "What about you two? How come you're so weedy?"

We told him our stories, which didn't take long. Then we sat quiet for a bit and shared a beer.

"So here we are, three orphan boys gettin' by in Australia," Lenny said. "No thanks to that lot at St Wilfred's."

"Too right, mate," Stanley muttered. "All that stuff about God and what do they do? Beat the livin' daylights out of us for years, then dump us without a penny."

Lenny and Stanley talked on, their voices bitter as they remembered the things that had happened at St Wilfred's. I tried not to listen. I knew they were right. Most of the priests had been pretty hard on us, and a few had been monsters. But I didn't like to face up to the fact that the grown-ups who were supposed to look after us hadn't really cared. It would be like thinking that God himself didn't care, and that was just too much for me to deal with.

"Did you ever hear from your brother, Bert?" Lenny asked after a while.

I felt sick as I realised I hadn't thought about my brother for weeks. A picture filled my mind of Frank's pale, wet face, the last time I'd seen him on that awful night as the road split in two.

"No," I said. "Father McTavish said we had to make a clean break."

"You don't have to do what he says any more, mate," Stanley said.

"I suppose not," I said. I hadn't thought of that. Suddenly I was desperate to find out where Frank was, so I could write to him. I would have to return to St Wilfred's, and stay there till they told me where to find him.

"I'm thinking of signing up for another cattle drive," Lenny said. "You boys could come with me."

"No thanks," Stanley said. "Chasin' loads of dozy animals across the outback for months on end ain't really my cup of tea. I've got a good job right here."

Both of them turned to look at me. The sun was setting, and it cast a golden glow over the dry, dusty land. It was beautiful. But I wasn't a farmer. I was a city boy at heart.

"I'm off to … Perth," I said, coming up with the place on the spot. It was the nearest big city. I could make my way there after I'd been back to St Wilfred's.

"Let's keep in touch, then," Stanley said. "You're both as ugly as sin, but you're the only mates I've got. Maybe we can meet up again one of these days."

I set off for St Wilfred's the next morning. I didn't want to arrive like a bushman down on his luck, covered in dirt and dust after a long walk. So I used the little money I'd saved to buy a ticket on the mail coach.

But it didn't make any difference. Father O'Flanagan refused point blank to give me Frank's address in New Zealand. He wouldn't even let me speak to Father McTavish.

There was nothing I could do, so I headed to Perth and got a job as a labourer on a building site while I worked out what to do next. A year later I was in Adelaide, in the south, where I did all sorts of jobs. A year after that I was in Melbourne in Victoria, the biggest Australian city I'd seen so far. I was fed up with the endless heat and the dust and the sun, so I started trying for a job in an office.

It took a while, but by Christmas 1913 I had one at last. I was a clerk in the offices of a big shipping company. I hadn't forgotten Frank – in fact, I was sure my new job would help me track down my little brother.

But it would soon be 1914. My freedom wasn't going to last much longer.

CHAPTER 6

Work to Be Done

The tram was packed and noisy – everyone was talking about the news of war from Europe. Huge, dark clouds filled the sky over Melbourne and a brisk wind threw a spatter of rain against the tram windows as I went into town to meet my mates for a beer.

Even after 8 years in Australia I couldn't get used to the idea that August was a winter month. It felt odd, like the year was going round the wrong way.

I'd been thinking for a while that I was still a Pommy at heart. "Pommy" was the Aussie word for someone from Britain. Sometimes it was said with a smile, but I'd heard it used as an insult too. Lots of Aussies still thought of Britain as "the mother country", and they were proud to be part of a great Empire. Others didn't have a good word to say for the country where I was born.

I listened to the talk around me on the tram. I knew I should be worried about the war that had broken out. Germany had invaded Belgium and France. Then Britain and France and Russia had all declared war on Germany and Austria, and so Australia had done the same. But I had other things to worry about. I'd spent the last few months trying to track Frank down in New Zealand and I had got nowhere.

Working in a shipping office had been useful, at least to start with. I knew all the routes Frank could have been taken, and the most likely one would have been to Auckland in New Zealand's North Island. Frank would have been sent from there to an orphanage, maybe in Auckland itself.

I couldn't afford to go to New Zealand, so I found out the addresses of all the orphanages in the country and wrote to them. Most of my letters came back with "Return to Sender" scrawled across the envelope. If anyone did bother to reply, they refused to tell me if Frank had ever been there. Perhaps they wouldn't know where Frank was now anyway – he'd had his 16th birthday a year ago. The Church would have turfed him out, too.

That all added up to one thing – a complete blank. I had no idea what to do next. Finding Frank seemed impossible.

I got off the tram close to the Town Hall. All the streets were crowded and noisy, and the Town Hall was covered with huge Union Jacks and Australian flags, and other flags too – French and Belgian and Russian. A brass band was playing in City Square. All the band wore dark green uniforms, and soldiers mingled with the crowd.

My mates Jimmy and Bill were coming out of the pub as I arrived.

"Here he is!" Jimmy laughed and he put his beefy arm round my shoulders. He was big and sandy-haired, an Aussie born and bred. "Sorry, mate, you've missed your chance of a beer," he told me.

"Why, what's going on?" I asked. More men came out of the pub and pushed past us.

"What's going on, he says!" Bill said, and he laughed too. "Don't you read the papers, Bert? Come with us!"

Jimmy and Bill turned me round and frog-marched me back to City Square. I went along with them, curious to see what the fuss was about. The band was still playing and an army officer was standing on a table that someone had dragged out into the square. A crowd gathered round the officer, waiting for him to speak.

"Ladies and gentlemen, the Empire is in peril!" the officer called out. His voice boomed across the square and a deep hush fell over the crowd. He had them in the palm of his hand. "At this very moment," he said, "the savage Hun is ravishing gallant little Belgium! Thousands of innocent women and children have been killed! It is our sacred duty to protect the world from the German war machine ..."

"Blimey, mate, have you swallowed a bloomin' dictionary?" a man yelled. There was a great roar of laughter. "Get to the point!" he shouted. "We're here to join up, not listen to you!"

"I'm glad to see some of you are full to excess with war-like zeal!" the officer boomed. There was a grin on his face, and the crowd laughed even more. "I can also see I don't need to give you any more of the speech I prepared. All I'll say is that anyone who wants to do his bit in the fight to save the world from the Hun had better join up sharpish. The war might be over by Christmas and you don't want to miss it!"

Most of the men in the crowd pushed forward, and I felt a powerful urge to join them. Another officer climbed onto the table and started to talk about glory and honour and adventure, but I wasn't interested in any of that. I only needed to hear the part about women and children being killed. I would fight to stop that happening.

Only one thing held me back. My search for Frank. I might never find him if I joined the army and went overseas. But my search hadn't been going well, had it? Maybe I ought to accept that I would never see my brother again. And at that moment the war seemed more important. The Empire wouldn't ask us to do our duty if things weren't serious.

"So what's the verdict?" Jimmy asked. "Are we in or not?"

"I'll give it a go," Bill said with a grin. "What about you, Shorty?"

That was their nickname for me. I didn't mind – it was pretty accurate. I was just five foot six in my socks.

"I suppose you'd better count me in too," I said. "Someone's got to keep you idiots out of trouble. Can't tie your own bootlaces without help."

Moments later we were inside the Town Hall. A sergeant showed us where to go, and we entered a large room. There were long tables at one end manned by more officers. Long lines of men stood waiting.

At last I found myself in front of a plump, middle-aged officer. He asked me my name, age and other details, then he wrote everything on a form without looking up. He handed me the form, waved me away and yelled "Next!"

Then a brisk army doctor asked me about any illnesses I'd had, measured my height and chest, and checked my teeth and feet.

"You'll do," he said. "Report to Broadmeadows tomorrow."

PART 3
RECRUITS
1914–1915

CHAPTER 7

They Gave Me a Gun

Broadmeadows was home to hundreds of new recruits. There was an enormous army camp there – long lines of tents pitched as far as the eye could see.

Our training began before we even had uniforms or rifles. We did endless drills, marching up and down while sergeants yelled at us to turn left, to turn right, to turn back again, to stand to attention.

Stanley and Lenny both wrote to let me know they'd joined up too. It felt good to know we were all in this together. I soon realised that many of the volunteers at Broadmeadows had also come from Britain. Many had been in the British Army before they came to Australia, and quite a few were ex-officers.

Jimmy nodded at one of the officers as we marched past. "I bet his grandfather was the judge who sent my Irish granny here in the first place," he muttered.

"Didn't know your granny was a convict," Bill said. "Should have guessed."

At least the officers seemed to know what they were doing, as far as training went. The camp was chaos to begin with, but bit by bit things got sorted out. By the start of October we had our uniforms, with Aussie slouch hats with the rising sun badge on the pinned-up side. We had rifles, too, pretty good ones – brand-new Lee-Enfield 303s, the same as the British Army.

Next we were organised into platoons, companies and battalions, and we were told we were part of the "Australian Imperial Force". A couple of weeks later we marched through Melbourne to the harbour where troopships were waiting. It wasn't far from the office where Jimmy, Bill and I had worked. Brass bands played and a huge crowd cheered us off on the first leg of our long journey.

They told us that the troopships from Sydney, Brisbane and Melbourne were heading to the harbour at Albany in Western Australia. The plan was to meet there and form a convoy to cross the Indian Ocean. It was the same journey Frank and I had made 8 years before, but in the opposite direction. I felt like I should have "Return to Sender" scrawled on my back, like my letters to New Zealand.

I was pleased to hear that New Zealand was also sending soldiers. But the Kiwis arrived after us – "Kiwis" was what we called New Zealanders. At last the ships sailed out of the great harbour to form the convoy – 30 Aussie troopships in three lines, ten New Zealand vessels in a line behind them.

It was a spectacular sight and I knew I would never forget it. The sun was shining and I was leaning on the rail at the back of our troopship with Jimmy and Bill.

"Hey, look at that beauty!" Jimmy murmured as a sleek grey warship steamed past us at speed. Its sharp bow sliced through the sea like a blade.

"That's the HMAS *Sydney*, the pride of the Aussie Navy!" Bill grinned. "I wish I'd joined the Navy. All the nice girls love a sailor!"

The convoy was protected by British and Australian warships. There was even a battle cruiser from the Japanese Navy – Japan was an ally of the British Empire. But my eyes were drawn to the Kiwi troopships instead. Frank was too young to be on one – Kiwis had to be 19 to join up and fight overseas. But I couldn't help thinking that somebody on a New Zealand ship might know my brother.

I didn't get the chance to ask. Some of the officers – the "brass-hats" as I had learned to call them – visited other ships, but the soldiers were stuck in our "floating tin cans" for the whole journey. There was a bit of excitement when the brass-hats thought the convoy was about to be attacked by a German ship, but that didn't happen. The sweltering days on board passed with more training, lots of training, always training.

At the start of December 1914, we steamed into the Suez Canal. The plan was to sail across

the Med and carry on to France, but then our orders changed. Now we were to stop in Egypt and do even more training. It was clear that the fighting in France and Belgium hadn't gone too well. The Germans had almost taken Paris, and the war wouldn't be over by Christmas.

The convoy docked in the city of Alexandria, and we took trains to Cairo. We were crammed into the carriages and we gawped at Egypt as it flashed past the windows. It looked like the Bible pictures we'd seen in the orphanage. There were palm trees and camels … and we even saw the Pyramids.

Our battalion made camp not far from the Pyramids. For the first couple of weeks in Egypt, we were busy. We did lots of shooting practice and fought mock battles. We slogged across sand dunes with full packs and spent long afternoons listening to dull talks about the war. Then at last, a week before Christmas, we got a day off.

"It's time we had a look round the city," Jimmy said. "Should be interesting."

That wasn't the word I would use. I'd never seen anything like it. Cairo was an enormous, sprawling city. We walked along narrow streets that were crammed with carriages and buses and trams and people – and most of them seemed to be yelling. There were beggars everywhere, many of them blind and diseased with missing limbs. But we also saw hotels and restaurants and cafés full of rich people.

It was a city of soldiers, too. Britain controlled Egypt then, and lots of British soldiers roamed the streets. That day we took a ride in a small horse-drawn carriage that the British called a "gharrie". We looked for things to buy, haggled with shop owners and tried the local food and drink. As we trundled along the packed streets, we saw drunken soldiers fighting, and once we saw the Military Police dragging them away.

"Come on, I could do with a beer," Bill said. He pointed to a café on one side of a square. "This place looks all right."

Jimmy, Bill and me sat at a table outside and we ordered beers from the waiter. There was a group of soldiers at the table next to ours. They had New Zealand flashes on their uniforms,

and they talked and laughed with strong Kiwi accents.

"You all right, Bert?" Jimmy said. "You look as if you've seen a ghost."

I was staring at one of the Kiwis, and he was staring back at me.

"I ... don't believe it," I murmured. I felt like I was in a dream. "Frank?" I said. "Frank?"

The Kiwi knocked over his chair as he stood up. His face was white and hard with rage.

"Hey, watch it!" one of his mates yelled.

It was like the soldier didn't hear him. He turned his back and strode away across the square.

CHAPTER 8

Started All Over Again

I sat frozen for a second, and then I jumped to my feet. Jimmy called out, but I didn't hear what he said. I broke into a run and caught up with the New Zealander just before he vanished into the crowds. I grabbed his arm and spun him round. The two of us stood in the square, in the midst of the noise and the people, and we stared at each other for a very long time.

It was Frank.

He was no longer a little boy. He had grown much taller than me – broad, fit and strong. His hair was darker than it had been, but his eyes were the same. I could see our mother's face in his, and I felt a sharp pang in my heart.

"It's me," I said, at last. "Bert. Your brother."

"I know who you are," Frank said. "And I want nothing to do with you."

All I could think was how odd it was to hear my little brother speak with such a deep voice. Then his words sunk in.

"I don't understand," I said. "I thought we ..."

Frank's face twisted with anger and contempt. "What did you think?" he jeered. "It's been eight years. Eight ... years."

"I know that," I said. "I've been trying to find you. Frank ..."

Frank sneered. "You didn't make a very good job of it, did you?"

Relief flooded through me – I could explain. "It wasn't like that," I said. "They wouldn't give me your address, so I wrote to all the orphanages in New Zealand."

"I never got any letters," he said. "How do you explain that?"

"The priests must have kept them from you," I said. "They said it was best if it was a clean break. But now we've found each other, Frank, so ..."

"So what?" Frank's voice was as hard as the look on his face. "You and I don't have anything to say to each other. Just leave me alone."

He turned and strode off again.

I stood and watched him go. After a long few minutes, I turned and went back to my mates.

"What was that all about?" Jimmy asked. "You got something against our Kiwi chums? You've scared the lot of them off."

He nodded at the next table, which was empty now.

"You're clearly terrifying, Shorty," Bill joked. "To Kiwis, anyway."

My face was numb. "Thought I knew the bloke," I said. "But I was wrong. Let's get out of here."

We went to a few more bars, but I was in no mood for a drink and I left my mates and returned to camp. I spent the rest of the day in the tent on my own. Frank had knocked me for six. I had been imagining this day for years. Never did I think it would happen like that.

Frank hated me. I lay on my camp-bed, brooding and sweating in the heat. I went over and over what had happened all those years ago. Was it my fault? Was there anything I could have done?

What did it matter? I'd broken my promise. I'd promised Frank we'd always be together and that I'd always look after him. And I hadn't kept my word. I had let my little brother down.

I didn't speak much for the next few days. I did the training I was supposed to, but nothing more. Jimmy and Bill tried to cheer me up, but I turned my face away.

One afternoon I was sitting on an empty ammo box, brewing tea on our Primus stove.

"Hey, Bert, you've got visitors," Jimmy said.

I looked up – and saw Stanley and Lenny grinning at me.

"G'day, Bert," Stanley said. "Seems we've arrived bang on time. I'm gasping for a cuppa."

"Hope you've got some sugar," Lenny said.

It was good to see my old friends. I felt a bit of the weight lift off me.

I gave them mugs of strong, sweet tea and we talked. Stanley was in an infantry battalion, and Lenny was in the cavalry, the famous Australian Light Horse. The two of them had met up a few days ago and set out to find me as soon as they could. Jimmy and Bill joined in our chat and, before long, everybody was getting on like a house on fire.

"Thank God you two have put a smile on Shorty's face," Bill said. "He's been walking round with a face like a slapped arse for weeks."

"He always was a moody so-and-so." Stanley laughed. "What's up, Bert?"

I wasn't going to tell them, but I realised I didn't want to hold it all in any more. So I told them about Frank, and how he had walked away from me.

"Bumping into you must have been a shock," Stanley said. "Frank probably needs a bit of time, that's all."

"Stanley's got a point there, Bert," said Lenny. "It's not every day you meet your long-lost brother. And I bet you're even uglier than he remembers."

"Hey, look who's talking," I said, and I punched him in the arm.

I felt a bit better now, thanks to my mates. I decided to leave Frank alone for a while, give him some time to get used to the idea of having

me around again. Then I would look him up – I knew where the New Zealanders had their camp. I would take it easy, try not to spook him, let him get to know me again.

Then it hit me. Frank was only 17 – too young to be in the army. Lots of boys lied about their age so they could enlist. That didn't bother me before, but it did now. I didn't like the idea of my little brother getting hurt, or worse.

Christmas came and went, then January. A few times in those weeks I set off to find Frank, but thought better of it. It was still too soon. And while I was fretting about Frank, everyone else was getting bored and restless, and that led to trouble. Some of the British officers thought they could give orders to Aussie soldiers, which didn't go down well with the lads. There was plenty of bad feeling, and fights and flare-ups with the locals.

"It's a good job we're getting out of here soon," Jimmy said one day.

"What?" I said. "You heard something?"

"Yes," he said. "I talked to a bloke at HQ and he says we're not going to France. We're fighting

the Turks instead. The plan is to knock them out of the war."

"Didn't even know they were in it," said Bill. "So where are we going?"

"Some place I'd never heard of," said Jimmy. "It's got a right funny name."

It was Gallipoli.

PART 4
ANZACS
1915–1919

CHAPTER 9

Sailed off to Gallipoli

We found out more one evening a few days later. A Colonel came to talk to our platoon. There was a hundred of us, sitting cross-legged on the sand while the officer stood in front of us. The Pyramids behind him were outlined in silver moonlight and a cool wind whispered off the desert.

"You'll be pleased to hear we're going into action at last," said the Colonel.

"About blinkin' time too," somebody called out, and everyone laughed. That was the Aussies for you, always cheeky to anyone giving them orders. But there was an edge to their laughter that I recognised. A lot of the blokes felt the way I did – half scared, half excited.

The officer smiled, then he did his best to explain it to us.

It was complicated, and I didn't understand it all. I got that Turkey was in the war, on the other side. Turkey controlled the Black Sea – and that meant that Britain and France couldn't send help to Russia, our ally against Germany.

Gallipoli was a piece of land sticking out into the sea south of Istanbul, the capital of Turkey. The Allies had tried to attack Istanbul with warships, but none had made it through. So now the brass-hats were sending troops to Gallipoli to turf the Turks out of that piece of land.

"There's no point shipping you off to France or Belgium when you're already in Turkey's back yard," the Colonel said. "The good news is that Johnny Turk is no fighting man. He'll surrender as soon as he sees you storming up the beach."

It was going to be a massive operation. The Aussies and New Zealanders would only be a small part of the total force landing at Gallipoli. The Colonel told us we had a new name too – the Australian and New Zealand Army Corps, or ANZACs for short. Most of the other troops would be British and French, and we would be supported by a whole fleet of warships.

I was relieved to hear we would go in first. The Kiwis – and Frank – would only go in when we had got the place secured.

"Lucky beggars," Jimmy said, with a nod to me. He knew how I felt about Frank. "It'll all be over by the time the Kiwis arrive!"

That was my hope too – and that I'd still be around when my brother came ashore.

Later, I wrote Frank a letter. I told him I was sorry and I wished him all the best, but I said I would respect his wishes and stay away. To tell the truth, I couldn't face the thought of him walking away from me again. But I felt better when I'd written the letter – if anything happened to me, Frank knew that I cared. Bill took it over to the Kiwi camp for me.

CHAPTER 10

Lambs at the Slaughter

The next couple of weeks passed in a blur. We spent days loading stores onto trains – food, ammunition, all sorts of equipment – to go to Alexandria where the ships were waiting. We cleaned and checked our rifles, we sharpened our bayonets, we filled and emptied and re-filled our packs. We studied maps of where we would be landing.

At last the day came when we got on the train and set off. A crowd of Egyptian children ran beside the carriages, yelling and waving.

"Gallipoli! Gallipoli!" they called out. Then they laughed and drew their fingers across their necks, as if they were telling us we were going to die.

"Charmin'!" Bill said. "How do they know where we're going?"

"Everybody knows," Jimmy said. "It's in all the papers."

"Hang on a minute ..." I said. "So the Turks know about it too?"

I felt very uneasy. Wasn't our attack on Gallipoli supposed to be a secret? I told myself the brass-hats must know what they were doing. Perhaps letting the Turks know was all part of the plan.

Soon me and my mates were back on a troopship, part of a huge convoy heading north across the sea. We passed rocky Greek islands dotted with white houses, and stopped on a warm and sunny day at a great harbour on an island called Lemnos. We transferred to British destroyers, then we set off north-east, heading for the Turkish coast.

We reached the coast in the early hours of 25th April. The moon shone above us, and I could see the dark mass of land ahead. Men lined up in silence all along the side of the destroyer. Big nets hung over the side and, when the word was given, we climbed down to smaller boats waiting below. It was hard with a full pack and a rifle, and men slipped and whispered curses as they went, but we all made it without any accidents.

Our boat was crammed – 40 men squeezed together. The men on the other destroyers were doing the same. 36 boats in total. Almost 1,500 men.

"Good luck to you, Shorty," Bill whispered. "And to you too, Jimmy."

Our boat jerked as they began to tow us to shore.

The moon had set and the sea was as smooth and glassy as a black mirror. I peered into the darkness ahead, and strained my eyes to see the beach. After a while they stopped towing and the sailors on the boat started to row us in. It was an eerie moment – the only sound was the quiet splash of oars dipping in the water.

Then a funnel somewhere spewed out a bright shower of sparks, and somebody swore. The words echoed across the sea. A crackle of rifle and machine-gun fire erupted from the land and bullets buzzed and whined and smacked into the wood of the boats – and into the men sitting in them.

I saw a soldier leap overboard in panic. His heavy pack pulled him down like a stone into the dark water.

The sailors rowed on, faster and faster, and soon word came that we'd reached shallow water. I scrambled out of the boat and gasped as I plunged up to my chest in the sea. The shock of the cold made me lose my footing and I went under, but strong hands pulled me back up. Jimmy and Bill dragged me onto the beach.

"Come on, we need to find cover!" Jimmy yelled, and we stumbled forward, making for the shelter of a cliff.

There was more light now, a beacon shining somewhere above. Already the beach was littered with dead bodies and wounded men begging for help. The rest were running and dodging, searching for cover like Jimmy, Bill and me.

The Turkish fire grew even more intense, and then the destroyers opened up with their 4-inch guns. Bright flashes lit up the sea and shells from the guns exploded at the top of the cliff.

"Well, boys, this is what I call a real welcoming party," Bill said.

Then his head jerked to the side and he fell face down on the sand.

He was dead.

CHAPTER 11

Rained Us with Shell

The 25th of April 1915 was the worst day of my life, even worse than the day Mum died or the day Frank and I were separated.

I saw men I knew wounded and killed in so many terrible ways – drowned, shot, blown to pieces, turned into mincemeat by red-hot splinters of metal from shrapnel shells. Bill's wound had been clean in comparison – the Turkish bullet had left a single ragged hole behind his ear.

It was utter chaos – brutal and bloody and awful. We found out later that we should have landed further north, on a wider beach where the cliffs weren't so high. All the units got mixed up and we were cut off from our officers. Most of us decided our best bet was to head inland and attack the Turkish defence. But our maps turned out to be useless. The land was a tangle of rocky ravines and ridges, ideal for snipers.

But we kept on. We scrabbled up the cliffs in search of those snipers. We threw grenades, then finished the job with bayonets. We fought all day, killing and being killed, the stench of death thick in our throats. While the fiery ball of the sun sank into the sea behind our backs, we fought on. We hadn't taken much of Gallipoli, but our orders were to hold what we had.

And what we had was a place we called Anzac Cove.

A month later, and things hadn't changed much at all. There was constant shelling and sniper fire from the Turks, and sudden attacks when they charged down at us with guns and bayonets from the cliff tops. We were jumpy, dirty and ragged from lack of sleep and decent food.

"I could murder a roast dinner and a cold beer right now," Jimmy said.

"Me too," I said. "A roast dinner would do me fine."

We were standing on the fire-step of a trench at the top of a ridge. The Turkish trenches were only 50 yards from us, half the length of a football pitch away. Sometimes you could hear their soldiers talking to each other. There was rocky ground between the lines – No Man's Land. It was uneven and full of shell-holes, in between the trenches and their strings of barbed wire.

That was in front of us. The view behind was pretty amazing. Dusty land sloped down to the beach of Anzac Cove and the calm sea below. Soldiers trudged up and down the narrow paths that zig-zagged over the rocks. Mules carried boxes and bags from the great heaps of supplies on the beach. From this distance the soldiers looked no bigger than insects.

Beyond the beach was the sea, sparkling in the warm sunshine that filled the blazing blue sky. Dozens of warships sat at anchor, and boats bustled between them and the beach. As I watched that day, a cruiser fired at the Turks further inland, and the roar of the guns was followed by the distant *crump* of explosions.

I could hear the rattle of the Turkish machine-guns, the *crack-crack* of rifles answering.

Just then Stanley came down the trench.

"G'day, boys!" he said. "Thought I'd pop over to see how you're all gettin' on. I've even brought you a present."

"Let me guess," Jimmy said. "A first-class ticket out of here?"

"No such luck, mate." Stanley grinned. "I'd have kept that one for myself. I got you this instead." He pulled a tin of bully beef from the pocket of his baggy shorts.

"You beauty," Jimmy said. "I was wondering what to have for dinner."

We squeezed into a shallow dugout in the side of the trench and brewed some tea, then talked and ate our bully beef sandwiches. We were a proper sight – more like tramps than soldiers. Our boots were thick with dust, our shorts and shirts filthy and ripped, and we were alive with lice that kept us scratching day and night.

"You heard from Len, Stan?" I asked. It had been hard to deal with Bill's death, and then

Lenny had nearly copped it as well. The Light Horse had left their horses in Egypt and come to fight in the trenches with us. Len's trench had been hit by a shell that killed a couple of blokes, and took off both his legs at the knee. He'd lived – just – but what was left of his legs was a mess of infection and he'd never ride his beloved horses again.

"I got a card from him," Stanley said. "He's in hospital back in Cairo."

"Glad to hear it," Jimmy said. "Who knows, he might even see a doctor there."

The brass-hats had been so sure that the landings would be easy that they'd only laid on a few doctors at Anzac Cove and on the ships, and the nearest hospitals were in Egypt. And the Turks had turned out to be terrific soldiers, brave and determined to defend their country. Thousands of our men had been wounded, and many had died for lack of a doctor. I hoped that wouldn't be the case for Len.

In fact, the whole thing was a bloody mess. I'd trusted the brass-hats, but they had been wrong about everything. The more I thought

about it, the crazier it all seemed. What was I doing there, invading another country, putting myself in the line of fire, seeing my mates blown to bits? It seemed that I was cursed to be sent from place to place by idiots who liked giving orders, but who didn't give a damn for me or anyone else.

Stanley interrupted my thoughts. "Saw your brother this morning," he said. "He seems all right."

Stanley's trench was next to the New Zealanders, on the left of Anzac Cove. I'd asked him to keep an eye on Frank for me.

"They've got a proper cushy billet there," Jimmy said.

"No such thing as a cushy billet at Gallipoli, mate," said Stanley.

He was right. The Turks made sure of that.

At dawn the next day the Turks launched more attacks. Two days of heavy fighting followed, as the Turks swarmed forward in wave after wave. We cut them down as they charged. I stood on the fire-step beside my mates, firing my rifle until the barrel was too hot to touch. Shells howled overhead like wailing demons, and the ground around me rocked with every impact.

On the third day, things eased off – except on the left. The noise of battle there grew even louder, and a great cloud of smoke rose over the trenches.

"Sounds like the Kiwis and Stanley's lot are taking a hammering," Jimmy said.

I didn't say anything. I couldn't take my eyes off that smoke. As I watched, another noise seemed to come from behind it – the sound of men yelling. Machine guns rattled away, warships fired shell after shell, then at last silence fell. I was desperate to know what had happened, but I wasn't supposed to leave my post.

"Don't worry, Bert," Jimmy said. "I'll cover for you. Just hurry."

"Thanks, Jimmy," I said.

I jumped from the fire-step and ran. The fastest way was down Shrapnel Gully to the beach, then along to the left and back up to the line. It took me ten minutes to get to Stanley's trench. It was littered with dead and wounded men, but Stanley was all right.

"God, am I glad to see you," I told him. "What the hell happened here?"

Stanley stared at me for a moment. "Bert, mate, I have some bad news. It's Frank."

CHAPTER 12

Blood Stained the Sand

I watched Stanley's mouth move but all I could hear was my heartbeat juddering in my ears.

Frank's platoon had launched a counter-attack, but then the Turkish machine guns had caught them out in the open. None had made it back to their trench. The chances were that they were all dead.

"Hold on a minute!" I said. "Chances? So Frank might still be alive?"

"I doubt it," Stanley said. "I'm sorry, mate. You've seen what a machine gun does to a bloke. And even if Frank's alive, you can't get to him in No Man's Land. The Turks will blow your head off as soon as they see you."

I ran off before Stanley could say anything else or try to stop me. I didn't even stop to think. I had no idea where Stanley's trench ended and the Kiwi trench began, so I asked the soldiers as I passed them.

"Yeah, this is Kiwi territory," a soldier said at last. "But there's not so many of us as there was this morning."

The Kiwis that were left were all staring out into No Man's Land, their faces blank with horror. I saw a short ladder in the bottom of the trench. I slung my rifle over my back, picked up the ladder and started to climb. Someone called out behind me.

"Stop! Where do you think you're going, you idiot?"

I paused and turned. It was a Kiwi officer, a Major, with a red face and a bristling black moustache. He was wearing a tie, his uniform jacket was buttoned, and his boots looked as if they'd just been polished.

"I'm going to find my brother," I said, and I carried on up the ladder.

"You're going nowhere!" the Major yelled. "You'll start the Turks off again if you go blundering around out there. I order you to get down."

I turned to look down at him again. His great ruddy face seemed to blur into the faces of all the other men in my life who had told me what to do. They had said they knew what was best for me and Frank – and where had that got us? All the way to Hell, that's where. Now this stuck-up brass-hat was ordering me to give up on my brother again. I'd had enough.

"Sorry, sir," I said. "I don't take orders any more."

Then I slipped over the top of the ladder and into No Man's Land. I crawled forward, low, scanning the ground, expecting to have my head blown off at any second. I soon came to the first bodies. They lay in a line where they had fallen, their dark blood staining the dry ground. I looked at each man, sick to my stomach at so much death, but glad every time I looked at a body and saw it wasn't Frank.

I found him in a shell-hole not far from the Turkish line.

I rolled over the rim as a sudden burst of machine-gun fire kicked up the sand behind me. The Kiwis fired in response, and for a few seconds the air above the shell-hole was filled with the buzz and whine of bullets. But I took no notice. I was only interested in Frank. My brother was lying on his back in the hole – and he was still alive.

The sun was sinking in the west and the shell-hole was filling with shadow. Frank's face was deathly pale in the gloom, his eyes were shut and his right arm was a mess of blood. But things could have been worse. Most men survived flesh wounds, unless they bled to death. I started to undo Frank's shirt so I could apply a field dressing. Frank opened his eyes and grabbed my wrist.

"It's me," I said. "I've come to get you out of here."

"Bert?" Frank said, his eyes wide. "I'm still dreaming ..."

He closed his eyes again and his grip on my wrist relaxed. I slapped his face. "Frank, you need to stay awake," I said. "Frank!"

"Leave off, will you!" Frank said, and he rolled away from me. He tried to sit up, but he groaned in agony and lay down again.

"You after a medal, big brother?" he snarled. "It's not going to happen. Bugger off, Bert. You never saved me before and I don't want you to save me now."

I stared at him, then I laughed. I couldn't help it. "You always were an awkward bugger," I said. "Wilful, that's what Mum called you. And she was right. It looks like this was a waste of time anyway. We're both gonna get killed now."

Silence fell between us for a moment. I looked up out of the shell-hole and saw the stars beginning to twinkle in the darkening sky. A machine gun rattled close by and another replied, almost as if they were having a conversation.

"Did you really write to all the orphanages in New Zealand?" Frank said at last.

"Every single one," I said. "It took me ages. Cost a bloody fortune in stamps, too."

"Serves you right," said Frank. "You shouldn't have let them send me there. You promised we'd always be together."

"What was I supposed to do?" I said. "I was only 12. A kid."

"I was only 9," Frank said. "I had no idea what the hell was going on."

Another silence fell between us, a longer one this time.

"Did the priests send you to another orphanage?" I asked. "Was it bad? I mean, did they treat you all right?"

"Tell you about it when we're in Heaven," said Frank. "I'm looking forward to it. Plenty of grub, and no priests."

I smiled. Frank was right – none of the priests I'd met had a hope of making it to Heaven. "Sounds good," I said, "but let's give that medal a go first."

"Same old Bert," Frank said. "You always were stubborn. But I can't stand up, let alone walk."

"No worries," I said. "You can go on my back, like when we were kids."

Frank snorted with laughter.

"Come on then," I said. "Climb aboard."

I dumped my rifle and got down on all fours. Frank shook his head, but then he did as he was told, and he climbed onto my back, groaning

with the pain of it. Then I set off, crawling up to the rim of the shell-hole and over into No Man's Land, making for the Kiwi trench in the dark. Frank's arms were tight round my neck, his breath warm in my ear.

It was tough. The rocks cut my knees and palms, and Frank grew heavier by the second. I kept stopping and starting, worried I might be heading the wrong way. But inch by painful inch, we crossed that awful place and I saw our lines at last. I called out so the men on sentry duty wouldn't think we were Turks trying a sneak attack.

"See, told you I'd look after you," I said, when we were safe in the trench.

"All right, don't go on about it," Frank said, a smile on his battle-weary face. "Better late than never."

CHAPTER 13

Wounded Heroes

I got away with disobeying an officer. I knew that stuck-up Kiwi Major would report me, but the next day there was another Turkish attack. The Major took a bullet in the throat and died an hour later. I felt bad about it, but my mates and my brother told me not to be so stupid.

"It's an ill wind and all that, Bert," Stanley said. "Just think yourself lucky, mate."

Frank was pretty lucky too. The bullet had passed straight through his arm. He lost a lot of blood, and his arm was broken, but there was no worse damage. I took him to the Casualty Station on the beach and stood over the doctor until he had dealt with him. Then I got him on the next ship for Egypt.

Frank spent the next two months there, and he was back in time for the big push in August

1915. Thousands more men died on both sides, but it was all for nothing. Me and Frank and Stanley survived, but our mate Jimmy was blown to pieces.

At last the brass-hats realised what we already knew – the whole Gallipoli campaign was a rotten idea. By January 1916 all the troops – Anzacs, British, French – had been pulled out.

A year later, me and Frank and Stanley were shipped to France with the rest of the Anzacs. We saw more trenches, more blood, more fire, and we lost far too many good mates. In October 1917, the Russians had a revolution and pulled out of the war. For a while it looked as if the Germans were going to win. But it didn't turn out that way. At last – on 11th November 1918 – the Great War was over.

On the day the guns fell silent, we had just taken a small French town. I stood there and looked at the bodies of dead soldiers covering the square in front of the church – our boys as well as Germans. At that moment I knew I would never go inside a church again. There was no

God for me. I would never believe in Church, or Empire, or government again.

I never went back to Australia. After France, we were sent to England. As soon as I saw the bridges across the Thames, I realised just how much I loved the old place. So, early in 1919, I left the army.

"Don't get me wrong, Frank," I said. "Australia is a terrific country, but this is where I belong."

"It's all right, Bert, I understand," Frank said.

We were at Waterloo with hundreds of other Anzacs who were going home. The train for Southampton was about to leave. I looked at the steam engine and remembered being here at this station with Frank, all those years ago.

"That's how I feel about New Zealand," Frank said. "I had a rough time there as a kid, but I just can't imagine living anywhere else."

We looked at each other and then the train whistle blew.

"Take care of yourself, won't you?" I said. "And write sometimes?"

"You bet." Frank grabbed me in a bear hug, then he walked away.

I watched my brother vanish into the crowd.

And the Band Played Waltzing Matilda

A SONG BY ERIC BOGLE

The chapter titles in *Anzac Boys* are taken from the song "And the Band Played Waltzing Matilda" by Eric Bogle. Eric Bogle is a Scottish-born folk singer-songwriter, who went to live in Australia in 1969. This wonderful, heart-breaking song about Anzac soldiers commemorates those who died during the Gallipoli Campaign and those who returned home. It is recognised as one of the best Australian songs of all time. Eric Bogle wrote the song in 1971, but it is so true to the experiences and feelings of the soldiers who fought in the First World War that many people think it was written at the time rather than more than 50 years after the end of the war. Eric Bogle wrote many other songs about soldiers and the war – you can read about them on his website.

Our books are tested
for children and young people by
children and young people.

Thanks to everyone who consulted on
a manuscript for their time and effort in
helping us to make our books better
for our readers.

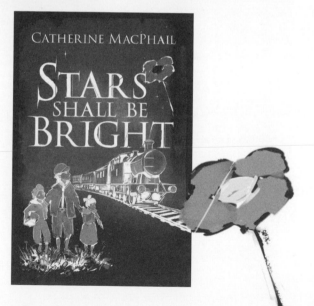

Over the Line

It's the proudest moment of Jack's life — his debut as a professional footballer. Now he has a chance to achieve his dream of playing for his country. But it's 1914 and the world is at war. Talk of sportsmen's cowardice leads to the formation of a Footballers' Battalion and Jack has little choice but to join up. The promise of a Cup in Flanders offers a glimmer of hope, but Jack and his team-mates will have to survive a waking nightmare if they are ever to play again.

Based on the true story of a sporting hero's experience in the trenches.

Tilly's Promise

When war breaks out, Tilly Peacock and her sweetheart Harry are keen to do their bit — Tilly as a nurse and Harry as a soldier in France. But the war drags on. Soon even Tilly's brother Georgie has been called up to fight, even though his mind is much younger than his body. Harry makes Tilly a promise to look after Georgie, but Harry and Tilly are about to find out that promises can be hard to keep.

Stars Shall Be Bright

When James, Belle and William's dad goes off to War and their Mammy dies, the three children have to move in with Mrs Carter. That's bad enough, but then Mrs Carter says they'll have to go into a Home. And so James, Belle and William set out for the Front to find their dad, on a journey that will go down in history ...

A stunning novel of World War One, inspired by the true story of the Quintinshill Rail Disaster.